Highlights **Puzzle Readers**

LEVEL 1
LET'S EXPLORE READING

Nick and Nack
See the Stars

By Brandon Budzi
Art by Adam Record

HIGHLIGHTS PRESS
Honesdale, Pennsylvania

Stories + Puzzles = Reading Success!

Dear Parents,

Highlights Puzzle Readers are an innovative approach to learning to read that combines puzzles and stories to build motivated, confident readers.

Developed in collaboration with reading experts, the stories and puzzles are seamlessly integrated so that readers are encouraged to read the story, solve the puzzles, and then read the story again. This helps increase vocabulary and reading fluency and creates a satisfying reading experience for any kind of learner. In addition, solving Hidden Pictures puzzles fosters important reading and learning skills such as:

- shape and letter recognition
- letter-sound relationships
- visual discrimination
- logic
- flexible thinking
- sequencing

With high-interest stories, humorous characters, and trademark puzzles, Highlights Puzzle Readers offer a winning combination for inspiring young learners to love reading.

This
is Nick.

This is
Nack.

Nick loves to **make** things.
Nack loves to **find** things.
They make a good **team**.

You can help them
by solving the
Hidden Pictures
puzzles.

Nick and Nack go outside.

"What do you see?" asks Nick.

"I see the moon," says Nack.
"But I do not see any stars."

"Where are the stars?" asks Nick.

Help Nick and Nack.
Find 5 stars hidden in the picture.

Happy reading!

3

It is almost bedtime.

Nick and Nack made a mess.

Time to clean up!

"Here is a towel," says Nack.

"More, please," says Nick.

"Here is another towel," says Nack.

"More, please," says Nick.

"Here are all the towels!" says Nack.

No more mess. No more towels.

"Look," says Nick.

"There is just a tube left."

"What can we do with the tube?"

asks Nack.

"We can make a telescope," says Nick.

"Then we can see the stars."

"How can we make a telescope?"

asks Nack.

"First, we need paper," says Nick.

"I can help find paper," says Nack.

Nick finds black paper.

Nack finds yellow paper.

"I found paper!" says Nick.

"We can wrap it around the tube."

"How will we hold the paper
on the tube?" asks Nack.

"We can use rubber bands!"
says Nick.

Help Nick and Nack.
Find 5 rubber bands hidden in the picture.

"Next, we need another tube," says Nick.

"I can help find another tube," says Nack.

Nick looks in the green bin.

Nack looks in the blue bin.

"I found another tube!" says Nack.

"Great," says Nick.
"We can put both tubes together."

"How can we make it even longer?"
asks Nack.

"We can put a cup on one end,"
says Nick.

Help Nick and Nack.
Find 5 cups hidden in the picture.

"Now we need stickers," says Nick.

"I can help find stickers," says Nack.

Nack finds spoons.

He finds shoes.

He finds stones.

He cannot find stickers.

"Here are the stickers!" says Nack.

"We can put the stickers on the paper," says Nick.

"Can we also draw with markers?" asks Nack.

"Yes!" says Nick.

Help Nick and Nack.
Find 5 markers hidden in the picture.

Time to make the telescope!

Nick wraps paper around the tubes.

Nack puts on the rubber bands.

Nick puts the tubes together.

Nack adds a cup to the end.

Nick adds the stickers.

Nack draws with the markers.

"The telescope is done," says Nack.

"Time to see the stars!" says Nick.

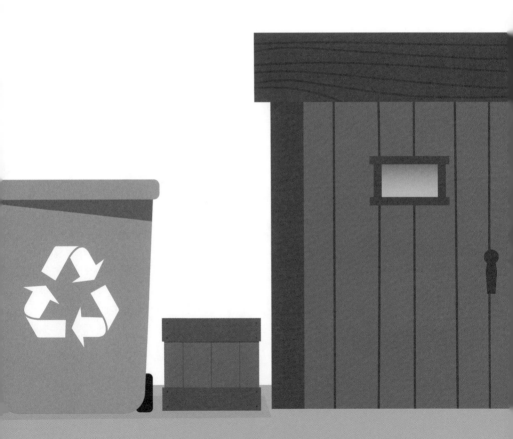

Nick and Nack go outside.

"What do you see?" asks Nick.

"I see the moon," says Nack.
"But I do not see any stars."

"Where are the stars?" asks Nick.

Help Nick and Nack.
Find 5 stars hidden in the picture.

Make Your Own TELESCOPE!

WHAT YOU NEED:
- Toilet paper roll
- Paper towel roll
- Paint
- Paper cup
- Black construction paper
- Pencil
- Scissors
- Rubber band

1 PAINT
- Paint the toilet paper roll and paper towel roll.

2 CUT
- Cut the bottom off of the paper cup.

3 MAKE THE STARS
- Draw a circle bigger than the mouth of the paper cup on black construction paper.
- Cut out the circle.
- Use a pencil to poke holes in the circle.
- Attach the paper to the mouth of the paper cup with a rubber band.

Try poking holes in the pattern of a constellation!

4 ASSEMBLE

- Fit one end of the toilet paper roll into one end of the paper towel roll.

- Fit the bottom of the paper cup onto the toilet paper roll.

Make more star patterns and attach them to the telescope to see different stars!

You can decorate the telescope with markers and stickers, or you can leave it plain.

5 LOOK

- Hold the telescope up to the light as you look through it. It will look like you are looking at the stars!

Nick and Nack's TIPS

- Gather your supplies before you start crafting.

- Ask an adult or robot for help with anything sharp or hot.

- Clean up your workspace when your craft is done.

For information about permission to reprint
selections from this book, please contact
permissions@highlights.com.

Published by Highlights Press
815 Church Street
Honesdale, Pennsylvania 18431
ISBN (paperback): 978-1-64472-192-6
ISBN (hardcover): 978-1-64472-193-3
ISBN (ebook): 978-1-64472-238-1

Library of Congress Control Number: 2020933667
Printed in Melrose Park, IL, USA
Mfg. 09/2020

Craft instructions by Elizabeth Wyrsch-Ba
Craft sample and photos by Lisa Glover

First edition
Visit our website at Highlights.com.
10 9 8 7 6 5 4 3 2 1

This book has been offically leveled by using the
F&P Text Level Gradient™ Leveling System.

LEXILE®, LEXILE FRAMEWORK®,
LEXILE ANALYZER®, the LEXILE®
logo and POWERV® are trademarks of
MetaMetrics, Inc., and are registered
in the United States and abroad. The
trademarks and names of other companies and
products mentioned herein are the property of their
respective owners. Copyright © 2019 MetaMetrics,
Inc. All rights reserved.

For assistance in the preparation of this book,
the editors would like to thank Vanessa Maldonado,
MSEd, MS Literacy Ed. K-12, Reading/LA Consultant
Cert., K-5 Literacy Instructional Coach; and
Gina Shaw.